Say Goodnight

Say Goodnight

TIMOTHY LIU

COPPER CANYON PRESS

ACKNOWLEDGMENTS

The poems in this book first appeared in the following publications: *American Voice, Asian Pacific American Journal, Bellingham Review, Caliban, Chelsea, Confrontation, Denver Quarterly, Folio, Gettysburg Review, Grand Street, Green Mountains Review, Harvard Review, Heart Quarterly, Indiana Review, Iowa Review, The Journal, Kenyon Review, The Nation, New England Review, Paris Review, Ploughshares, Plum Review, Poetry, Poetry East, Poetry International, Provincetown Arts, The Quarterly, Quarterly West, Salmagundi, Shenandoah, The Threepenny Review, Urbanus,* and *Willow Springs.*

"The Storm" and "Vespers" first appeared in *Seven Hundred Kisses: A Yellow Silk Book of Erotic Writing* (HarperCollins, 1997).

"Say Goodnight (IV)" was reprinted in *The 1997 Anthology of Magazine Verse and Yearbook of American Poetry* (Monitor Book, 1997).

"Poem" was reprinted in *Poems for the New Century* (Aralia Press, 1996) as part of the Hand of the Poet Exhibition from the Berg Collection at the New York Public Library.

Kudos to Bruce Beasley, Christopher Davis, Linda Gregg, Sam Hamill, Robert Hass, Jane Mead, Rodney Phillips, and Michael Wiegers.

Copyright © 1998 by Copper Canyon Press

The publication of this book was supported by grants from the Lannan Foundation, the National Endowment for the Arts, and the Washington State Arts Commission, and by contributions from Elliott Bay Book Company, James Laughlin, and the members of the Friends of Copper Canyon Press. Copper Canyon is in residence with Centrum at Fort Worden State Park.

LIBRARY OF CONGRESS CATALOGING-IN-PUBLICATION DATA
Liu, Timothy.
Say goodnight : poems / by Timothy Liu.
  p. cm.
ISBN 1-55659-085-7
  1. Gay men – Poetry. 1. Title.
PS3562.I799 S29 1998
811'.54 — DDC21   98-8918
                   CIP

COPPER CANYON PRESS
P.O. BOX 271, PORT TOWNSEND, WASHINGTON 98368

AS ALWAYS, FOR CHRIS

"La mia vita, l'universo, per un detto."

"Sie Sagen, daß die Liebe bitter schmecke…"

Contents

III.

IV.

I.

That Room in Which Disaster Played a Part

A bed behind four walls that framed a world.
Our neighbors who did not open their doors
are gone now, broken sprigs of jasmine
strewn about meticulous lawns at dusk.
August almost over. Still we lie, one on top
of the other. I tried to draw a mountain
and a wooden flute with music coming out of it
but it turned out wrong. So many flowers
igniting in that garden beyond the mind –
four walls and a door we called the future.

Say Goodnight

It is better to be alone. Tree and sun
as icons beside a house with windows
that never close. No hills. It seems
this was all the lovers could imagine –
broken crayons strewn about the table.

First Day

The children set out for school, no books
in their packs, a sycamore they have ignored
all summer aflame like the gilt-edged
pages of a Bible magnified under glass.
Yes, the early deaths of autumn, pitiless
as the broken neck of a goose flung

across a country road, downy tufts afloat
in weed-choked ponds like a ghost armada –

What slow migrations congeal in the blood
of carcasses smouldering on compost heaps
out back, rows of blighted cornstalks
hacked down by a greased machete. How night
trundles forward on the backs of toads –

the farmhouse on the hill supine, its windows
sheeted under a thick mail of frost.

And the calls of wild geese at dawn rupture
the thin sac of sleep where arms and legs
crouched fetal float in the residue of some
forgotten dream – the glassed-in kitchen
all astir with the smell of pig fat smoking
against the rim of a cast-iron pan.

The Garden

We were after crevices, whatever God had
commanded the fire to leave untouched –

a bed of charcoal lines where lovers
lay supine, the moon's raw face appearing

and disappearing. Night gathers her brood
of stars as open-throated vases cry out

for roses – our grief an urn on the head
of a woman who turns away from the well.

That Summer

We buried my mother's bird, a parakeet
sealed inside a shoebox. No more singing.

Nor the sound of broken words she had
taught it how to speak. Like that book

on Blake I found in the garage with pages
torn out of it. What is touched by loss

is sometimes made more sacred – that grave
exhumed at last by a neighborhood stray.

Treasures on Earth

What no one wants. Coin by coin,
we forget our burdens, our eyes drawn
upward to a white sky, an icy cake
whose candles the world has blown out.

A Vision Made Out of Corrugated Tin

A head of Jesus framed
in a squatter's shack. You stood there brooding
with the radio off.
Wildflowers wilting in the yard and supper
burnt again. No cleaver
to break the neck on that squawking bird,
I turned to violence –
a hardwood board nicked with cuts while a game
of chess continued on
in some back room late into the night.
You say forty prayers –
storm-torn nests exposed in branches that reach
for winter. What remains
for me? Forty games with the same opponent
who will not let me leave
that crooked kitchen table where we sit
till I admit defeat.

Stray Dogs

weaving across the divided road
as sheets of ice come down.

Hoard kisses while they last.

Try to hold steadfast to bodies
that dissolve into song –

Crepuscule with Mother

Stacked up on a changer, that slow
molasses drawl at sixteen RPM
hysterical at seventy-eight –
     some golden oldies in our heads
          for decades after those dead musicians
     were put away. Even after Father
folded up the Ping-Pong table we hid
     behind when Mother started smashing dishes.
          Her voice had several pitches
     others hardly knew. At parties, she served us
tuna sandwiches, stuck parasols
     in our punch. She tried. Still we lost our faces.
          Me reading spines on worn LPS
     just to avoid her gaze – Williams, Evans,
Monk – names I had already begun
     to store inside my fingers those evenings
          at the piano, a glass breaking
     here or there, Father wrestling the cleaver
out of her hands. She only knew one piece
     by heart – *Crepuscule* – and it seemed to calm her
          even when it sounded wrong.

Pietà

On a plane heading east, children playing
solitaire. If each of us seeks the face

of a god whose looks we know will kill us,
why build a house of cards up in the air

and call it heaven? *Choose ye this day*
whom ye shall serve, the prophet said,

and I remember the stranger who whispered
Crivelli into my ears while we stood

before the painting. Before my mother took
more pills. The gilded cards she gave me

each had the same masterpiece on it.
We both held up a fan of cards, our eyes

veiled behind an agony – a mother and son
unable to look into the other's face.

Old Diary with a Page Torn Out of It

Words that formed in a child's mouth
as bees thrummed inside the marriage hive.

Voices are not created equal. Yet who am I
to close the book that lay beside my bed
unread for years? My father's scent

faintly on those sheets where I had slept.
Our flesh has a memory of its own.

Now we want it back, stripped of tragedy.
Old hives teeming into the new where wings
fall through those weathered slats –

each room of our lives rearranged
whenever a stranger entered it.

Birdsong Forever in That Childhood House

Three children playing "Around the World," the ball
getting heavier till it got too flat to shoot with –

    White snake in a canvas sack ready to strike,
the tip of my pencil stuck inside the hole
      of a sharpener, slow click of classroom clocks
after school where I had stood erasing boards,
        chalk dust piling up on trays. Someone shouting

over beer that soaked into the grain of an oak floor,
Mother sinking lower into a tub filled with suds.

    The dog all summer pulling against a chain,
its paws marking circles in the backyard dirt,
      California orchards in fragrant bloom
when I met another boy named Tim, wondering
        if I had somehow lost my way – torn pages

from a notebook impaled on a broken branch, yellow
of the willow the only color for miles around –

    The sky's black veil falling. Boys inside a gym
learning how to let go more, fingers tracing
      an x where a cat's-eye marble had rolled under
the polished floor, discarded lambskin condoms
        snagged in the flowering trees – memory

like the woman on our block who touched everything
in her room before she died. In spring, the birds

    returned but their songs were heavier, those
sketches in my father's house merely footnotes
    to a life he never lived – each strand of hair
swirling down the shower drain like a prelude
    to some dirge old age perfects – a room

where no one waits at the end of the day,
loneliness equal to our desire to be alone.

    How strong it smells, the nights we go without –
paper stacked up on the desk, the wings within
    a fountain pen tearing free. Down Amherst Road,
three children playing "Around the World." I turn
    to look at a winch that creaks on a flatbed

truck hauling timber thicker than my waist. My God –
is death at work so early in the afternoon?

Last Day

How each of us grows tired of this world,
our heads a cradle of raucous birds
greedy with disregard. Neither snowdrift
blown onto our porch nor bootprints
leading away from the door can explain
our desire for distance. The body has
its limits. Still nothing to keep my hair
from growing down to my feet, ecstasy
in the sound of glass breaking somewhere
below. A kind of violence, a memory –
that smell of grass burning under snow.

Kindertotenlieder

Another fire dying down, the view from here
about to change – my father listening to Mahler
late into the afternoon, a scripture torn

from the family Bible floating upward on a bed
of its own ashes, unable to withstand

a child's magnifying glass. (As if a girl
could just lie down in the middle of the road
while her bicycle continued on without her…)

My father dreaming of a better world where girls
don't suddenly turn into a boat of flowers –

diamonds of safety glass strewn on a gravel road
where old men wander into the night to rest
their heads on bales of hay, the countryside full

of barns braced against the wind. (Tell us where
the rain has gone.) A woman closes her mouth

for forty years and we say the world is a place
charred by the sun, no moon or stars in a barn
where that truck raised high on concrete blocks

waits for a pane of tinted glass – a childhood
we almost had through which to view the world.

Strange Music

      Men have seen their own graves at the edge
of clinic beds, afraid
      the watches strapped to their wrists are nothing
         more than faces on clocks
      still ticking in a childhood house. To kneel
before a dying lover
      is to know those calendars yellowing
         against a wall. Sometimes
      men stop eating. Just like that. No taste
to revive their tongues again.
      Bells linger in the air long after
         pigeons fly up into
      the afternoon, yet nothing endures
longer in the mind
      than that echo of what we might have been.

Two Men on a Swing Watching
Their Shadows Lengthen

Pruned back last winter, the grapevines
start to bud mid-May, the arbor still
too white with a new coat of paint.
Another robin crashes into the earth,
its carcass scattered by the blades
of a reconditioned mower. The swing
slows. You touch my knee, and I hear
the brass weights of a grandfather clock
steadily falling in that cottage where
we met, the season's first snow fresh
on the ground as hands ran up and down
a polished cherry cabinet built
to last. Like barrels of oak fermenting
in the dark. Is life nothing more
than two men on a swing watching
their shadows lengthen? No more music
stirs in that room, only a window
overlooking a yard with a birdbath
filling up with snow. Touch me again
even while an ant on a rotten stump
struggles to carry a petal underground.

The Storm

Black ants crawl in the sugar bowl,
me no longer checking the mail.

How stars in the window shift as I
begin to forget. Cricket song

instead of your voice. The fire
we started nothing more than ribs

of ash on an iron grate. A time
when we spoke. Come to me in a dream

where I don't appear. Closer still –
as if love were more than a fever

of moths crowding a lighted square
moments before the power goes out.

After the Storm

Renewed by morning air now pouring in
through a torn screen, we wake to dawn's

cold invasion, so many birds outside
it sounds like a tape of Brahms on cue

or review, that unrest of something
always searching. Once my heart rate

slowed when I fell in love, altering
the scale of pitch. All my Callas CDs

left me dissatisfied, particularly
the sinewy tessitura of Turandot's

opening aria, "In Questa Reggia," stretched
to breaking. It took weeks for my ear

to recover a sense of proportion – her
ghost-like footprints trailing through

the house as though it too were a stage
dissolving to an oversong of sparrows

under the eaves where caws of crows
punctuate the cries of cats glassed-in

all winter. We cannot help but sleep
in late as the sound of another early

westbound train rumbles through town,
carrying off what remains of our dreams.

Some say the world will burn when Jesus
comes again, Lord of ash and all things

passing. The empty page asks nothing
but our failures—a dawn full of birds

on branches smeared with soot. You said,
We are a hacksaw cutting through a cage

of bone. You tell me how Hsu Chi Mo
went down in mountains covered with mist,

how words go out of print. Yet fascicles
sewn-up by Dickinson's hands survive

the grave. Not Amherst. Nor the heads
on pennies buried in the earth we found

while planting bulbs—one with the date
of my mother's death and another with

your birth. Or was it merely a dream
with wings flying too close to the sun,

a book out of which the congregation
sings – their bodies more naked now

sitting upright in burnished pews than
all the men and women who have slept

in our arms? How the room grows vast
each time you turn away, no marriage

lasting longer than a thousand nights,
passion itself a dying swan, a story

without wings. Neither coins stacked up
on a granite stone nor prayers recited

in an unknown tongue can turn back
the breaking day – glistening haunches

that spring out of the earth in one
clean arc from birth door to the grave.

Last Day

With all the windows closed, I go on
sleeping. Winter losing shape.
Empty vases left in every room
of the house. Those backyard bulbs
releasing a company of spears –
each tulip's guarded flame
a color only the gardener knows.
Will he wake me as he passes through?

II.

A Valentine

A room within my body where the broken
vowels are, where the unsleeved arms of men
lead me back to the galley of a gutted
ship turned on its side – an empty heart-shaped box
washed ashore like some belated valentine
unclaimed by the sea – beaks still wet with krill
perched on rotted pilings that line the docks.
(The mills of Pittsburgh bore me, Provincetown
undid me.) Was your touch mere tease or prelude
to some obstinate paradise that I could not
enter? Perhaps I alone must smear these
petty reveries across the page, the dawn's
diaphanous wings now plummeting into some
far corner unfathomed by the waves slow
susurrus – that flaming shirt stripped off your back
a salt-stained flag still floating on the bilge
where the clang of weights refined your body
into something the world could love, each of us
harboring what the other lacked: a wilderness.

Herring Cove Beach

Fenced-off from the world, men lying
on their backs, the curves of their sex gleaming
    under spandex briefs – the way life
        desires to unfold – a child
        dismantling rosehips, spilling
a secret hoard of seeds as we wade out
    into the Atlantic undertow –
        tides whisking the glasses off our faces
    while a nimbus of men on shore
suddenly lose their hard-won definition
    on a stretch of virgin sand where
        children hide in the shadows of the dunes –
    a boatload of whale watchers
far out at sea, drag queens flailing bangled
    arms as if they were going down,
        throwing out flowered hats to see how long
    they would float – the men on deck
now cheering them on for it came to them
    like grace – something that would save us
        when our bodies failed.

North Truro

Late summer at its height falls faster
than a makeshift kite, cormorants

flying toward a boat-bespeckled bay,
dry kelp flaking off our soles like bits

of burnt confetti. Down unmarked trails
on rental bikes eaten through by rust,

we cruise between those rippled dunes
where shirtless men jack off, our eyes

tethered to wads of tangled string
wrapped around a bone. No local catch

can quicken the coals we fan at dusk
where fiery kites in erratic schools

swim through the air on invisible lines—
raw hands reeling in a dying wind.

At Limantour

Memory failed where shore birds wheeled
against the pull of the moon, children
ankled in ropes of kelp leaping up
at dusk. Had we come so far for this,
so close to the edge of our ruined maps?

Aperture

A moon obscured by clouds rocked my stomach
as we sailed into uncharted waters –

unshelled shrimp left on a plate, my palate
shot. Unable to help, you laughed.

Then voices singing in a foreign tongue
as I hung on to your wrists, sheets of ice

glazing the chairs and Christmas lights
on deck. Our poses remain in the slow burn

of photographs, fingerprints eaten away
by time as we hold on to that image

by its edges. What else can we do but strike
a match against all we cannot save

off Padre Island – so many men gone overboard
on a promenade silvered by the moon.

For Those Who Do Not Dream

Watermelon seeds in the belly of a woman
four thousand years old. What survives.
Her apparent hunger. My father said
that men dream best when they go to bed
without food. Early this morning, you
called, and we ate each other to the rind.

Say Goodnight

Trunks of charred pines rooted to the rocks.
Women laid to rest in fields they dug up

when alive. Who will come to warm themselves
beside the hearth where dogs huddle close
while a man in a Shaker chair nods off

into sleep? We only can see a little smoke –
those chimneys blackening an evening sky.

No Other World Than This

A blade of grass springing out of time's crevasse –
desire four-horsed as it drags its empty chariot

through the marketplace looking for cuts of meat.
The body's want beaten down with wildflowers twined

through links of heavy chain, some crucial scene
now taking place in a prison outside of town –

the hum of burnt-out filaments in an overhead bulb
no good for late-night reading. Behind the door

is another door with a square of glass framed in it,
a face appearing where the surface is scratched –

your own face hovering there like someone wanting in
while couples all across the country call it quits.

Nocturnes

❧ *Chelsea*

A roll of quarters to enter a world
where the only words we seem to know are
suck that big dick and *open my hole* –
the silence broken – those studs on screen
floodlit, blood-engorged as we grope
for whatever we can get, some disco
soundtrack pulsing all around those vials
of over-the-counter ecstasy.
Who can blame such men who only long
for touch?, roses sold on sidewalks
soon replaced by venereal sores blooming
in the cracks of jack-off caves
hewn out of stone, the hot and hung enacting
pagan rites on monitors embedded
in a plywood maze – cum-stained stalls
no wider than an elevator shaft
filled with groans. Let men be more than shades
entombed in underground vaults that sprawl
throughout the city, death's perfume
spilling out of every orifice –
so many offices with lights left on
this late into the night as we stroll
down spiral stairwells into some back room
bricked up with boxes of video hunks,

lurid smiles plastered onto bodies
hammered by time's sure blow – the buddy booths
below already packed with patrons who
empty out worn pockets of all their change.

⌒ Eighth Avenue

No matter how we ask our bodies to behave,
the affair begins and ends in the mouth – the wife

who turns in her sleep hardly dreaming of asphalt
newly washed where taxis lumber into dawn

with their final fares, the two of us on a couch
in back of the Barracuda with Chelsea boys

whose eyes are glued to monitors while models work
their way down ramps between shots of Technicolor

dick – Björk and Kitchens of Distinction drowning out
every other word we speak till our lips become

a silent movie without a script, you and I
needing a change of scene – umbrellas opening

down streets without a destination, only rain
converting hotel awnings into temporary

shelters, an old man fishing out his wedding band
from a sewer grate. No other signs of life

along this avenue, only the "Love Ewe" flashing
on a dim marquee above that neon storefront

filled with a flock of inflatable party sheep
while you descend into the subway stop alone.

∿ *Fire Island*

Shards of glass embedded
in the sand where the party

had broken up, only love's
detritus – embers faintly
glowing in a blackened hole,

condoms smeared with shit
discarded through the weeds.

∿ Joshua Tree

Each of us locked inside our rooms
with nothing to say. At Yucca Valley,

the Joshua trees stood apart as poets
do from the world, our footholds

caught in a chain of granite crevices
shadowed by the moon. The sex gone

from our marriage, no adventure left
in a motel bed. Where is the door

that leads into the wilderness inside
of us? The master said, *Reading*

ten thousand books is not as good as
walking ten thousand miles, taking

no thought of those elderly couples
sipping teas that rattle with ice,

a scorpion scuttling across the floor
of a pool that had been drained –

Let the cry of a hawk stand in for
rain that will not fall in a forest

of two-by-fours rising out of cement,
our lives fenced-in by desert roads

that always lead us back to a room
full of people who butcher the air

with words – so many lies and lullabies
nailed down behind the bedroom door.

∾ *Latin Quarter*

You were not there. Not under mansard roofs
where pigeons had taken hold, the sky
a bolt of secondhand cloth studded
with winter stars, Orion the one
constellation I still could name
on a dead-end street – Guarneri violins
being burned for fuel as the smell
of Camembert and roasted lamb
drifted through that quarter whose windows
and doors were barred. Those were the streets
Bellini walked, his "Casta Diva"

a turning away from society
ladies wrapped in chiffon gowns, hair spritzed
with a saffron glaze while marzipans
teased their tongues – my own reflection
now vanishing from storefront glass.
But where were you when the waiter
sauntered through that beaded curtain
with monkfish floating in a dish of cream,
after-dinner kisses passed around
like a plate of petits fours, bird cries
caught in the folds of a season
that would not last? Even a pyre
is nothing more than a passing hour –
a bulletin that the heart's mute theater
has lost its patron. So I dine alone
in an empty house, this open bottle
of cassis wine poured without applause.

Last Day

We crane our necks into that stillness
where petals dust the sill—a woman

reclining on an iron bed where days
surrender to shadow while a sheet

snakes under her hips. And if the body
is nothing more than a room waiting

inside another room more barren than
before? Perhaps too much to feel

entirely loved without that memory
of lost books lying open on the grass.

Reading Cavafy

How many pages did the poet turn
before dozing off, knowing
he would never find what had been
lost? Those roses on the table
cast a shadow in the shape
of a darker rose, flattened there
beside the book. He sleeps
alone where the scent remains.

Reading Tu Fu

No blueprints left in the house.
Only a cardboard tube we used
to support that kitchen table

with a missing leg. Excavations
the size of Xian now spread out
before our feet as we picnic

on ancestral grounds, the rain
already tearing at the paper
lanterns. We dine in *happi* coats

on the family quilt – patchwork
of regret – raising a toast
to whatever survives the night.

Reading Lu Chi

Moonlight touching all eight corners
of a room where antiquity flowered

late – eyes cast down to hand-thrown
jars cracked with a celadon glaze

while ashes falling from a mountain
of books return at last to the source.

Apostasy

Those voices from below roiling up
around our ankles,
                    scalloped edges
gouging at our ankles in the sea foam –
succumb   succumb
                        the moon a trophy
hung in heaven, nothing but pages
scattered on the floor
                        where a pen lies
on a desk for forty years in fear
of faded passages
                    marked in red –
the Word of God in my father's house
a monolith
                that grew too heavy
for us to lift – a brigade of ants
marching over torsos
                        cast in bronze
outside the chapel door, a fountain
smudged by the lips
                  of passing strangers
as we wait for the next god-body
to appear: how we want
                    that ghost-Christ

kneeling over there, hands outstretched
on a burnished pew,
                    the cross not loved
as symbol but as wood and nail –
that iron song
              as our bodies flail.

The Bait

Adam fishing in a lake,
his genitals floating
in the reeds – cut off
at the waist, a double-
minded lure suspended
between two worlds, Eve
rising up from under.

New Colony

An epidemic, checked in one locality, breaks out
in another – Separatism's seed an expedition
fit away in a shallop so shot to the huckle-bone
the greater halfe dyed in the genrall mortality.
Some survived, only to endanger their lives, consume
their own estates by any ungodly course – pilgrims
leaving the natural use of the woman, men with men
working that which is unseemly, the Privy Council
notified of the arrests *to make provision*
if ther be cause, by deprivation of member, or life.
Madhouse buggers disguised as magistrates engaged
in the business of making fustian for lusty men
under the command of Myles Standish: one entangled
in a deer-trap made with a noose attached to a bent
tree, another stripped buck naked – made to perform
unnatural rites, his mind far gone like a cargo
of beaver skins for the voyage home, considerable
tracts of land outside the Town Square polluted
by a single acre on the south side of the brook
where boys were seen cavorting. *And to new evills*
arissing, or new dangers, to apply new remedyes
as is fitting: how those Indians blanketed
with the pox lay down on beds of ash left behind
by fagots smouldering in the pits, a slow smoke
rising through those woods for centuries after.
Even the treaty with Massasoit could not account

for such desire *to propagate the gospell in diverse parts of the world altogether unmanured, and voyd of inhabitants,* or so we had been told by rectors who assured all would emerge from the font reborn.

The Prodigal Son Writes Home

I want to tell you how he eats my ass
even in public places, Father dear,
the elastic round my waist his finger hooks
as it eases down my crack (no classified
ad our local paper would run, I'm afraid,
        but that's just as well).
We met in a bar that's gay one night a week –
teenage boys in cages, men on the floor,
but that's not what you want to hear, is it?
How he noses into my cheeks on callused knees,
lip-synching to the rage of techno-pop,
        that ecstasy of spit.

He's after me to shit into his hands.
What should I say? (I told him I'm afraid
he'd only smear it across my wide-eyed face,
hard as it is to tell you this.) How plans
have gone awry is more than apparent here –
        this sty he calls a home
tender as a mattress filled with our breath,
our sex unsafe. *Oh stay with me*, he croons,
my eyes clenched shut, head trying not to flinch
as he makes the sign of the cross on my chest
with a stream of steaming piss, asking me
        if we were born for this.

Blackout at the White Swallow

We swivel in our seats as pool balls crack
between bruised cheeks on monitors flanking
both sides of the bar – boytoys drinking out

of doggie bowls while men in leather masks come
to mount their holes. Shots of Jack and numb
refrains of "Dancing Queen" rein our senses in

as strippers primp and preen – so many throats
emptied of all their smoke. Why should we love
old trolls who prey on jocks too sweet to hold

a grudge? Weathered faces drown in liquor
troughs while meat is herded across the floor –
nipple rings and barbell studs piercing tongues

the new stigmata even as we settle for men
slumped over billiard tables where latex
fists are warming up behind a beaded curtain –

His Anus as Ventriloquist

"Your glance disrupts my ease, faces
painted onto asymmetric Asmat shields
    imported from Irian Jaya –
        relics to avenge those refugees
    hunted down by Klansmen just off
the coast of Galveston – razor burns
    round nipples nicked by double blades
        that attempt to resettle the body's
    wilderness. Another rice queen
nursing at my breast – a conquistador
    whose milk-toast smile noses into
        my ass meat's sweet abyss as natives beat
    their drums, navigating canoes
downriver in search of sago palm and game,
    the harpoon's arc zeroing in
        on some object of desire kneeling
    beside an ivory bowl – memory
baiting all of us with waterlogged pages
    from a book fished out of the sea."

III.

Forty Years

Work boots in the basement thrown against
a wall. The garden dies in the mind –

nasturtiums entwined on a chain-link fence.
The gods he carried nothing but dried

crusts. That vintage bottle on the table
crushed more each time he hammers it.

A Calendar (With Months Torn Off)

Nailed to the wall. Anything to lift
our burdens out of bed as sunlight

yellows the leaves. Audubon's birds
one year and Mapplethorpe the next

to call the lost sheep of our hours
in at the end of the day – wayward

flocks growing fewer as black wolves
vanish into those hills at night.

Two Men in a Rest Home
Looking Back at Us

One unable to speak, the other
slumped over in a chair – jaws working hard
    to oil a mouth that only family
        would kiss. We are given one body only,
    youth a faded mask that never fit.
Would we get in bed with them, trying to love
    what we will become – spent passion
        like some recurring dream we carry
    to the grave? A calendar bearing
Michelangelo's slaves – such eternal folds
    of flesh touched by mortal hands.

Ten Floors Up

No one enjoying the view, the stereo on
full blast. Biscuits on a saucer
dusted with sugar. Violetta wasting away
on a mono recording: La Scala, 1955.
Is there nothing else for us to do?
My lover crying harder, pointing
to the corner where he had crouched
for three days thinking death was better,
me not talking, sick
of some invisible hand pinning us there.

Elegy

Your brother dies and you are jumping off
a bridge ninety feet higher than before –

bungee cords tied around your ankles.
You said it felt safe. Peter died. All eyes

on his lover who slept in a chair. Family
came and went. Was it just last week you came

ten feet from hitting the ground? Happens
all the time, funerals louder than an Irish

wake – everyone blitzed. No one mentioned
AIDS. Had there been more rage at the flames

that licked each cell of his body clean,
his cock reduced to cinders, all evidence

of a life destroyed, we'd believe he died
with honor – no need to write this elegy.

Two Men on a Bench Watching the Light Die Down

Rollerblades careening down concrete
as we face the ocean, the scent of star jasmine
stronger than dusk – our heads a trespass
against the stillness we embody. Must we
step out of modesty just to touch
the nipples of shirtless men bronzed by the sun
or follow trails of sweat streaking down
spandex shorts that lend desire shape?
To undress those men is to hasten
what stirs inside our bones – an ocean within
that spills into this world from dark to dark.

Say Goodnight

Muted bells ringing inside my body
as I undress, thinking of that afternoon
a stranger pinned me down between the legs
of my mother's piano where we had been

rehearsing hymns that we knew by heart
as twin shafts slid through valves of spit,
pure grip rammed into bruised hips, the bench
mere plinth to the masterpiece we were.

A Baedeker

∽ *The Elgin Marbles*

How much we want to piece it all together –
folds of a stone skirt, flanks of centaurs
    rearing where the hooves are not. Fractures score
      and rift those fallen marble façades,
    slabs hauled out of history where the myths are
not entirely lost. The sculptors' hands
    did not survive. Torsos are enough, stone curves
      on those men and beasts so much alike
    we cannot tell where one begins, the other ends.
Such weight time carries forward on backs
    that labor, heifers lowing under barren skies
      hammer-blown by the rain. Piece by piece,
    poverty will triumph over all. The bread
that once fed multitudes has hardened
    into stone – Demeter with hands outstretched
      to Dionysus who leans on a staff
    now missing. If the gods are not immortal,
why reconstruct their temple? Myths
    need more mortal voices, or else the ones enthroned
      must forfeit all their power over us.

∼ At the Rodin Museum

Water pooling in the pleats of a bronze skirt
where caryatids glisten in the garden

after rain. Two men wrestling on a stone plinth.
No matter where we turn, the air greens

each body alike – the torsos of Pierre de Wissant
as ghastly as those figures jutting forth

from the Gates of Hell – time's slow verdigris
veiling them all in a luminous shroud.

From Vence

We break a basket of braided dough
where pigeons crown a stone Madonna smeared
    with excrement – a thirteenth-century font
        draped with moss more sacramental
    than a chapel's tile roof glinting
on the next hill over where a tour bus had
    released its air-conditioned faces smothered
        with tan from a tube – geriatric
    pilgrims packed into a stained-glass sacristy
tempting *our* instamatic restraint.
    Alas Matisse, known atheist, could not paint
        an icon. His stations of the cross
    only testify to what is possible
in our time – Virgin, Child, Patron Saints –
    each left without a face, abstracted gestures
        floating in a void where we
    who had gathered there could not afford
a silence equal to those rising
    squawks around the postcard rack, as if art
        could forgive us of all our sins.

∾ From Nice

A shingled beach receding into those
canvases of Dufy – regatta fleets

anchored to unearthly blue. Was art
the lure that brought us here

or life? Grind-organs buried under
dust in back of an antique shop

closed for good. Not a soul in sight
at azure's edge as day retreats.

～ *From Marseille*

Thousands of masts spear the sky, no water
to be seen in this old port, only sterns
    afloat on Marseille's cracked mirror – its war-torn
        skyline rebuilt again and again.
  A thirty-foot virgin gilded gold turns
her back on the flotsam and jetsam
    of La Canbierre – fleets of skirts and wedgies
        where a rack of lamb spins round all night
  in a snack bar run by a Greek, fat dripping
off that vertical spit like hot wax.
    Holy Mother, can three-franc candles stacked inside
        a blackened basilica make
  intercession for our disbelief, each flame
an unanswered prayer? Night slowly
    lifts her veil. Two sailors kiss each other's cheeks
        under canvas parasols painted
  with leaves, hawkers on the quai packing up
their trove. How dawn arrives on the wake
    of a motor-driven barge that's heading out
        to the chalk-white cliffs of Chateau d'If.
  Towels and masks by noon encrust those rocks
bezeled in the sea, bare feet dangling
    off a precipice – foam spray in the distance
        fanning out from a keel as sunlit portals

illuminate those cells where prisoners slept.
We paid our francs to be ferried here.
   Such pleasures last less than a day, forgotten
      loves graffitied under the arches
of the Palais du Longchamp, pigeons bathing
between the hooves of those granite bulls
      leaping forth from a terraced font, the water
         cascading down in ever-widening rings.
No lens could do this palace justice –
Leonardo, Michelangelo, Raphael
      chiseled into the North Wing's façade where
         twin spires instead of masts compete
with the Virgin's height, Marseille a belt of stone
constricting the horizon, each tile
      roof a mosaic of clay and soot – all weight
         and girth poised on the brink of commerce –
ships sailing across the centuries with slaves
in the hold, empires flaming out
      as the sun sinks into the world's burnished haze.

From Arles

Houses of stone shall not be spared.
Sarcophagi with lids blown off,

a trough of air where bones had been.
Rubble strewn on the Roman walks

of Alyscamps. You piss against
a fractured font while pigeons nest

high up those desecrated walls
where the icons have been dislodged.

❧ *From Barcelona*

Miró's phallus crowned with a crescent moon
in this public park we cruise, firecrackers
    igniting pigeons that all fly up at once –
        the sounds of Catalan ringing in the square
    as the curtain in that cardboard theater
falls on a city where men in soiled coats
    sell packs of cigarettes near kiosks
        peddling daily news and iced horchatas
    that wax our throats. How we want
to taste the new, trying to make talk
    in Padam Padam – phrase books in this gay bar
        useless – each of us arrested by a gesture
    or a look. To sleep with a stranger
on a Talgo train tonight with one moon
    shining over all of Spain, no language
        on our tongues but the sound of pigeons rising.

∾ Guernica

No tears in Picasso's final version, eyes
pulled earthward to the grave. How easy

to lose one's faith in his aesthetic –
iron blades where tongues should have been,

life splayed to the hilt. Yet we're moved
by a canvas void of color, no longer

deaf to a chorus of dismembered limbs
crying out from its two-dimensional cell.

Plaza de Toros

Fuchsia blooms fan out on the killing floor
as the bull breaks free, kicking, skidding
          across the turf, hoofprints tacking down a field
                    ringed with lines of chalk. As trumpets sound,
          padded horses ushered in by picadors
trot between those princely staves.
          The Prado was not enough. What lasts is the sound
                    of horns goring into wood, blindfolded
          horses tumbling sideways into dust. We are
mesmerized by a whipping tail, the sex
          flapping like an udder as the flanks heave – nape
                    of the feral bull lanced with a spear
          sounding another round of brass. All remains
sport until the hide is shawled with blood –
          banderilleros wooing death as bestial roars
                    echo through the crowd, six spikes crowning
          a neck with thorns. The matador appears
and I am bored by twitching nerves as bulls
          drop to their knees. Each time a cape is draped
                    across the back of another beast,
          a chorus of *"Olé!"* rises. Why this lust
for death, my thirst to see a human fall
          unquenched – performance staged right from the start?
                    Because we paid for it. To feast

on what is *here*, a carcass trailing blood
as its roped hooves are dragged out of the ring –
ourselves the broken body, the mythic form.

IV.

The Sign

Bird shit streaking down
the backs of Adirondack
chairs, a naked woman
sketching. Is the point
of art to know what hands
will do? For a moment
she looks up, then resumes.

Action Painting

A canvas we cannot stretch across the frame
nor staple down to fact: a ladder leaning

against an awning, workers pitching tar
on the roof of a church packed each week

with swine – a chain of pearls dangling
off the limbs of an artificial tree

where Boy Scouts gather in a tool shack,
jacking off to the sounds of Perry Como

on a karaoke machine – a televised priest
gesticulating wildly at the pulpit again.

Nothing but the Truth so Help Me God

Nine lamps in the shape of teeming censers
hung from a courthouse ceiling, forty
wooden chairs facing a video screen.
This is America. Jury duty
and the token fanfare of breaking
from our daily routines, men and women
with baskets of tropical fruit on top
of their heads. Justice for all and some time
off. Dionne Warwick in a floor-length gown
not singing. Trying to hook her fans instead
on the Psychic Friends Network: *Touch me*
not for I have not yet dialed that
900 *number.* America, talk
to me. The clock stops ticking, but someone
keeps on holding a microphone to our lips.

A Boston Fourth

Faces sludging forward on the esplanade
to where we are. What we are is energy –
    our bodies angled skyward as fading blooms
        parachute toward the earth, the crowd
    a spent militia – torn blankets left behind
as we march to the riverfront where
    tiny flares corkscrew up the sky to release
        delayed reports. The night gives up
    its ghost – wreaths of smoke crowning floral
cornucopias that spill a motherlode
    of fire onto both sides of the shore,
        hoarse voices bellowing out rote words
    learned in grade school that take on
meaning in a country of peace where
    thousands scream through the dark, waiting
        for that twenty-one-gun salute.

Ode to Bunker Hill

Song of burnt-out gaslights humming at dawn
as history retreats,
                the monument
not far from where we sit – two pigeons poking
their beaks into a spigot.
                   Morning comes
to the Training Fields like a pug who drags
its leash, chasing after
                 a tennis ball
some unseen hand has thrown. A neighborhood
gentrified by upstarts –
                song in the wood
of benches bolted to the ground, tar cans
filled with trash
             all smouldering from within.

Power

Half of the penis remains
    for a man whose dong had been bitten off
        by a dog, the organ extended

by cutting ligaments that attached it
    to the pubic bone, the public
        turning away from preop photos

of another member eaten out
    by cancer – two million men (ruined
        by birth defects, burns, and accidents

on the farm) still waiting for
    the pudendal nerve in the perineum
        to be reconnected for pleasure.

How else restore their dignity? – phallic
    disabilities our nation's silent
        agony. But what of men

who want a couple of extra inches
    for their own self-esteem, standing outside
        a clinic in Toronto

among boutiques, no sample large enough
          to estimate what constitutes
                    an "average" endowment?

Some say it's a power thing. Pure power.
          An impulse not to be resisted –
                    phobias in locker rooms

across the country. (Lorena Bobbit
          flinging her husband's manhood
                    out the window.) Some go through with it:

dysfunction and death the risk they take
          as they give consent – sex lives
                    reconstructed with rectus abdominus

myocutaneous flaps
          while a manicurist from Ecuador
                    (who claims her husband forced

anal sex on her) gets acquitted
          in front of courtroom cameras
                    in Manassas, Virginia: "Attacked

the instrument of her torture."

"An impulse that she could not resist."

"A world in which the biggest knife wins."

Billions Served

A cow without an eye? Not an uncommon sight
in stockyards run by the stocks we hold – cancer

eating out her eye, half of her face, and part
of her skull and brain. Better to have died

en route – pig sockets bleeding from electric
shocks that send them squealing down a steel sluice,

the ones not fit for meat left to starve – guts
bursting from the sides of a goat as maggots hatch

in the folds. How far now to the nearest fast-
food joint? Miles of tracks. Acres fertilized

with baby chicks ground up alive, the males no good
for hatcheries. Death's industry a sight

kept from our view where euthanasia's simply not
cost effective while the bull market rises –

a metal bolt now striking through the skulls
of newly stunned veals, conveyor belts starting up

as the hooves and heads come off whether or not
the throats are slit, fingers ground down to stubs

while families try to make ends meet –
a long line of workers as far as the eye can see.

Oasis

Just off the Jersey Pike we saw it –
the Walt Whitman Service Area – our bladders
    full, stomachs caught up in the rapture
        of a Roy Rogers burger – a self-serve fast-food
feast: long lines of men standing behind
the urinals, those sideways glances zooming in
    on a common need that brought us there.
        Some held back, others leaned into it as they shook
    and choked the last drops out (almost
satisfied), briefs and boxers anointed alike
    with a small wet stain, cigarette butts
        spinning round as piss streamed past rubber skirts.
    No pubic hair would fall unnoticed
on the lip of an unflushed john if Walt were here –
    father of unspeakable desire
        wherever two or three are gathered in his name.
    How those men kept filing in – truckers,
Boy Scouts, New Yorkers, bikers – no time it seemed
    to look for glory holes, to worship
        at the altar of a stranger's groin and taste
    the infinite while wives and lovers
rummaged through a bargain bin in search of tunes
    to play just once on a beat-up deck
        for the ride back – a hard pack of Camel lights
    and some change to spare on the burning
dash – none of us losing any time at all.

The Rand McNally Road Atlas

Boys in the backseat
jacking off, trying to hit
their favorite state.

Off I-80

Stands of sumac border that exit ramp
where the past erased itself, you behind
the wheel of a two-ton U-Haul packed
with all we owned. Iowa entered us, fields
pinned down by the weight of cornstalks
walling out the sky. The road thinned
to gravel. Then mud where wheel ruts were –
no sign that we had reached summer's end.
How to love this world where young and old
mill about a bingo tent, hot dogs served
on beds of sauerkraut while funnel cakes
flower in vats of oil? United Methodist
ironed on the faded tee of a man who shouts
*five in a row, four corners, the center
always free!* while a thirteen-dollar pot
kicks off the day. Less than life, more than
parade, a suspender hangs off the shoulder
of a Lisbon firefighter, bales of hay
blocking off the street where bathtub races
zigzag through the heart of White America.
Screams rising above Victorian rooflines
as metal egg-shaped cages on a Rock-O-Plane
tumble past treetops plastered to the sky –
the voice of God echoing through a town
where skins of burst balloons cry out
on a tepid afternoon. How lost we were

amid fields of corn, our wheels turning mud
where weathered barns loomed like bison
grazing on the horizon, the radio
fading in and out to a local gospel station.

The Presence of an Absence
in a Midwest Town

Crosses doused with gasoline hotter
than a mountain of books burning
on a Saturday night where ennui has
as many names as churches on the main
drag – dandelions across those lawns
with a worm curled up around each root,
the town's one signal light burnt-out.
A mother and daughter logging off
a screen left in the lap of a son
whose father was last seen cruising
Boystown. This too is America, two men
in bed reading late at night, dirt
beneath their nails as they ruminate
on a Klan Watch Report: *Nine Neo-Nazis*
slay two men walking hand in hand
down a Sioux City street. Should we
take up arms? Or vows of silence after
that order of Benedictine monks
outside Dubuque? No midnight runs
to the nearest Kum & Go without some
new threat. We deserve it, ministers
say, all of it foretold by doomsday
prophets, active Hate Groups dotting
a pull-out map of America like a field
gone wild – last year's harvest a ghost
of husks. Yet we wake each morning

to radio talk: an Anti-Smut Amendment
for children caught surfing the Net,
stiff fines imposed on porno stills
more accessible now than a single
page of the Gutenberg Bible ever was –
anyone with basic skills logging on
to get on-line with Satan (beaver shots
and dick controlled with a mouse), more
windows on those laptops than houses
still lit up this late into the night.

Poem

Late butterflies gliding through the air –

how else to begin without a mouth
full of pins? Life is more

than chrysalis. There are voices

in the earth, a vengeance you can taste
in all our crops. The monarchs

are dying out, some say whole streams

gone to rust that once meandered down
to Mexico. Our resident toad

returns no more. Only children

on the sidewalk writing stories in chalk
under blue pines dusted with wings

that flutter out of their lives.

Against Nature

Those bottled fruit flies in Bethesda
(darlings of genetic research
    for nearly a century) waste no time
        in getting down to business –
laboratory love gone awry
(Ward Odenwald and Shang-Ding Zhang
    bewildered at the males in circles
        who start to link up end to end
    with a frenzy once reserved for females –
winged conga lines parading
    inside those gallon-size culture jars,
        the buzz of homo love songs
    filling the air) – a single gene spliced
into this scene responsible
    for findings later published – a stretch
        of DNA on human x
    chromosomes said to affect our sexual
orientation according to
    the NIH whose flies may offer clues
        to the biochemical roots
    of lust, the Rev. Louis P. Sheldon,
president of the Traditional
    Values Coalition, already crying out
        for "reparative therapy"

to correct those defects nature has left
undone (the amino acid
        tryptophan wreaking havoc on the lives
            of flies), serotonin levels
        in the blood of Gorski's rats leading
to a study on human brains –
        dimorphic nuclei left in the hands
            of Simon LeVay, the calculus
        for the survival of our species
yet to be solved for straights or gays
        while furor in the media erupts
            into churches across the country –
        genetic tests to abort "abnormal"
fetuses the stuff of science
        fiction (for now) while flies and rats
            continue to get it on and on…

March on Washington, 1993

No friends we knew had died of *it*, Patient Zero
remote as Vietnam. We did not stop
at the War Memorial, too pumped up by the thousands
who thronged the Mall, children in the shade
with pinwheels in their hands, no wind, only the sound
of someone hawking ice cream from a cart
while twelve-foot squares of hand-sewn quilts parachuted
toward the earth. We ducked into the Hirshhorn,
Rothenberg's horses arresting sunburnt faces, each stroke
a thundering hoof. We envied that stillness,
something final. Achieved. Not a life cut short – early work
juxtaposed with the late until a correspondence
was revealed. Then we were back in the world, Ru Paul
rippling like a sequined American flag
onstage outside the door. And it was spectacular
even after the show – thousands of wasted
bodies packed into those Metro stations underground.

Two Men in the Hirshhorn Walking Hand in Hand

If the clocks in that room were to come
to a halt, they would hardly notice it –
Rodin's sirens hammered out of marble
till the agony shone through. Beautiful
in their ruin. Francis Bacon's skull
of an animal waiting in that green room
forever. Unmarred and beyond possession.

Easter, 1996

Meat hardly resurrects these days,
dear abattoir. Idyllic hogs
wallowing in the mud not part of this
reality – pork hocks cellophaned
on styrofoam slabs. Outstretched arms
cross enough for us to bear
but who comes now to hold this man
in his hour of dread? Eumenides
where those metonymical mouths grace
an unprimed canvas creased inside
a secondhand monograph? Keep
looking. *You have dined,* Emerson said.
Now face complicity. Brick by brick,
the walls must be disassembled
till the artist's carcass is reunited
with its shriek. What comes now
unbidden but meaningless words
to those who have resigned their parts
in the casual comedy? Merrill.
Monette. And all those stricken
voices sold off by the pound –
the dice-rattle lodged in our throats.

Strange Fruit

Spray-painted across a garage door.
No names to attach to the crime.

No cause for alarm – some lesbians
returning home to find their cats

still hanging from a coat rack
in the entry hall – Holiday's muted

voice echoing through the house
on that CD player left on repeat.

Ripened Fruit Pulled Earthward
to the Ground

No bread in the house nor birds
in the yard, a pale stone
with my name on it rolled up
to the door. The children
who knock this evening know
that I am done for, beg
to dig a hole in the ground
for next to nothing. How cold
and sweet the oranges are
as they arrive in boxes
fresh from that other world.

Say Goodnight

No kisses. Not tonight. Stand
before that folding easel
and sketch the cup, the saucer,
the china plate.
                    We shall eat
after all our labors. No doubt
the canvas will be torn to shreds
as quickly as a pencil rolls
off the crooked kitchen table –

and night with its call of trumpets
will sound in our ears as lovers
say goodnight.

Vespers

So many want to be blessed.
I only want to kneel in a quiet room.
To love what we have or not exist
at all. Nothing to help me sleep.
Only a scrap of paper slipped
into my hand: *Your body an ocean,*
a song without end. Votive candles
flickering in the dark that made us
larger than life: hip-thrust,
back-arch, mouth-grip, you on top
till we collapsed in the coiled
springs that came to rest. A chair
where you once sat. A bowl of fruit
neither one of us would touch.

About the Author

Born and raised in California, Timothy Liu was educated at
Brigham Young University and the University of Houston.
He has since taught at Hampshire College and was recently
on leave from Cornell College to serve as the Holloway
Lecturer at the University of California at Berkeley. Widely
published in such places as *Grand Street*, *The New York
Times Book Review*, *The Paris Review*, and *The Washington
Post Book World*, his poems and papers have been acquired
by the Berg Collection at the New York Public Library. He
is the author of two other collections of poetry, including
Burnt Offerings (Copper Canyon Press, 1995) and *Vox
Angelica* (Alice James Books, 1992). Liu currently lives in
Mt. Vernon, Iowa.

The typeface is Janson Text, created by Hungarian traveling scholar Nicholas Kis in the 1680s. The face, designed while Kis worked in Anton Janson's Amsterdam workshop, inspired revivals by both Merganthaler and Lanston Monotype in the 1930s. Adrian Frutiger and others at Linotype contributed to this 1985 digital version. The title is set in Carter & Cone's Big Caslon. Design and composition by Valerie Brewster, Scribe Typography. Printed on Glatfelter Author's (acid-free, 85% recycled, 10% post-consumer stock) at Bang Printing.